D1515039

Treetures

Meet the Mudsters

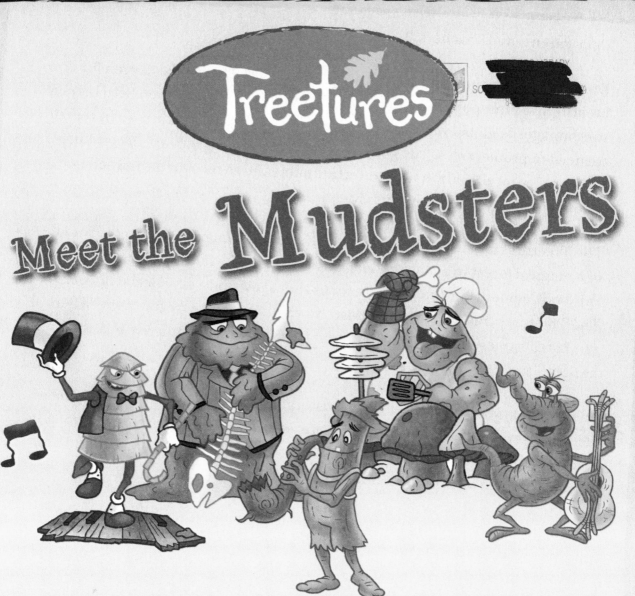

Based on the characters, art, and stories created by Judith Hope Blau

By Megan E. Bryant
Illustrated by Paul E. Nunn

Grosset & Dunlap

AMERICAN FORESTS
americanforests.org

A portion of the proceeds of the sale of this book goes to American Forests to help plant trees for forest ecosystem restoration.

Library of Congress Control Number: 2007040877

ISBN 978-0-448-44822-0   10 9 8 7 6 5 4 3 2 1

Dear Parents and Teachers,

Do you know how important trees are to the Earth? They make oxygen for us to breathe and filter pollutants from the air and soil. They may even help reduce the damages of global warming. Trees are our Earth's protectors, so in return we need to protect trees. The goals of the Treetures program are to combine environmental education with entertainment and to teach children science through friendly and funny fantasy characters.

The Treetures are tiny tree keepers who live inside a big oak tree in the middle of a magical forest in a place called Nutley Grove. The family of Treetures in this book comes from enchanted acorns that grow on a very special old oak tree. The Treetures travel all over the Earth to visit trees and care for them. When the Earth's trees are strong, other plants, wildlife, and people are healthier and happier, too.

In this book, you'll also meet the Mudsters. The Mudsters are a creepy gang of decomposers who hang out in the Treetures' magic forest. But, they're not all bad. Together, the Treetures and the Mudsters teach kids about trees and how to care for them and the environment.

After you're done reading this book, learn more about trees, the Treetures, and the Mudsters by visiting www.treetures.com.

Happy reading!

Very **TREELY** yours,

Judith Hope Blau, creator

P.S. **TREE CHEERS** for you! By purchasing this book, you're helping the environment. For every book sold, I will donate a portion of my earnings to tree planting and environmental education. In addition, as part of the Treetures publishing program, Grosset & Dunlap will donate money to American Forests, a nonprofit organization that helps plant trees for forest ecosystem restoration.

GLOSSARY

There are some important
words you'll learn in this book.
Here's what they mean:

BACTERIA (say it like: back-**TEER**-ee-uh): microscopic organisms that help break down matter during decomposition.

BARK: the outer protective covering of a tree trunk, and its branches and twigs.

COMPOST: rich soil composed of tiny bits of decaying leaves, twigs, and wildlife waste—the kind of soil you'd find in the woods.

DECOMPOSITION: when dead tree parts—like fallen leaves, branches, and wildlife waste—are broken down into simpler, smaller, mushier materials.

FUNGI (say it like: **FUN**-guy): organisms that, like bacteria, help break down matter during decomposition. Examples of fungi include mushrooms and molds.

HUMUS (say it like: **HYOO**-mus): a dark, rich part of soil that's full of nutrients and vitamins. It is the top layers of soil that are created when decomposition stops and there is nothing left to break down.

NUTRIENTS: vitamins, minerals, and other substances that trees need in order to grow healthy and strong.

ORGANIC MATTER: is made-up of dead plants, tree parts, grasses, and wildlife waste.

RESIN: a thick, sticky substance, full of good ingredients, that helps a tree make a barrier to fight off bacteria and fungi.

SAP: a sticky fluid made within the tree that the tree uses as food.

TRUNK: the middle of the tree that connects the roots at the bottom to the crown at the top.

The Treetures are magical creatures who live inside a big oak tree in the middle of an enchanted forest in a place called Nutley Grove. The Treetures care for trees all around the world. In the Treetures' magic forest, a creepy gang of decomposers hang out, too—they are called the Mudsters. Treetures need Mudsters and Mudsters need Treetures. Together Treetures and Mudsters teach kids like you about trees and how to care for them and the environment!

Here are the Mudsters you'll meet in this book:

Mud Meister

Mud Meister is a Soil Spoiler. He likes polluted places, soil erosion, and stagnant water. He also likes to bring pollution to healthy soil.

Humus

Humus is a Super Compost Chef. He enjoys eating and collecting dead roots, leaves, vegetation, and wildlife waste, which help make rich soil that's healthy for trees.

Crud

Crud is a Decayer.
He pretends to be part of a healthy tree to attract tree-destroying insects and diseases to openings and wounds in the bark.

Fun Gus

Fun Gus is a Mushroominator. He likes to hang out with his bad fungi friends and decompose healthy trees.

Root Snoot

Root Snoot is a Root Rotter.
He steals water from needy tree roots or drowns the roots with too much water.

Here are the Treetures you'll meet in this book:

Twigs

Sprig

Twigs is the Treeture Teacher.
He is very wise. He teaches Treetures
all about caring for trees and how
to help them grow.

Sprig is a Treedom Fighter.
He works to keep forests safe and healthy.

Chlorophyll and Chlorophyllis
are part of the Sunbeam Team.
They direct sunlight to leaves so the tree can
make its food and create oxygen.

Chlorophyllis

Chlorophyll

Rootie

Roothie

Rootie and Roothie are Rooters.
They care for trees' roots and
encourage them to grow.

Woody and Phloemina are Sap Tappers.
They care for the pipelines that bring the
tree food from the leaves to the roots, and
water from the roots to the leaves.

Phloemina

Woody

Blossom is a Tree Twirler.
She helps the wind, birds, and bees spread
tree pollen so that baby trees can be born.

Blossom

Mama Greenleaf is the
Keeper of the Crown. She watches over
the newborn leaves that grow at the tips of
the branches at the top of the trees. She also
watches over the Sproutlings.

Mama Greenleaf

Doc Barkley

Doc Barkley is a Tree Doctor.
He helps trees heal their wounded bark
and keeps them healthy.

Bugsey is a Blight Fighter.
He chases insects and bad bugs away
from healthy trees.

Stomper is a Compost Master.
He collects and directs leaves and debris to
the soil around trees. These leaves and debris
decompose and become dead organic matter
that forms a dark, rich soil called humus,
which provides trees with nutrients.

Bugsey

Stomper

Chip is a Sproutling.
Sproutlings are young Treetures
who are learning about trees. He recently
earned his green heart and loves helping out
all the Treetures with their jobs.

Chip

GOOD NEWS, BAD NEWS

Once upon a beautiful summer day—below the ground in the Mush Room, where the Mudsters lived—trouble was brewing! Root Snoot had some big news, and he couldn't wait to share it with the Mudster crew.

"What's all the fuss?" grumbled Mud Meister, the leader of the Mudsters.

Can you think of an area near you where the Mudsters could do some good decomposing?

Root Snoot's long nose waggled excitedly. "I was walking past that beautiful apple tree in Nutley Grove, and you'll never guess what I saw!" he exclaimed. "A cut! Right on the tree's trunk!"

"Nice work, Root Snoot," Mud Meister replied. "A cut in a tree's bark can make the tree weak—and that's when we can really do our dirty work. To the apple tree, my friends."

Since the Mudsters were *decomposers*, it was their job to turn dead tree parts, like fallen leaves, broken branches, and animal litter, into rich soil. But sometimes, they got a little carried away and latched onto a healthy, growing tree, which could lead to big trouble!

3

A MUDDY PLOT

"But what about the Treetures?" whined Crud. "They'll never get out of the way long enough for us to have our fun."

The Mudsters grew quiet. They hated to admit it, but Crud was right. It was the duty of each and every Treeture to nurture and care for all the trees. No Treeture would ever allow the Mudsters to harm the apple tree.

Then a sly smile spread across Fun Gus's face. "I have an idea," he said. "Let's throw a party at the Stump Dump and invite the Treetures. They love hanging out when we turn those old dead stumps into healthy soil. And while they're busy eating treats from Humus's Soup to Yucks Kitchen and listening to tunes from our band, DK and the Rotten Rockers, we can sneak off to the apple tree! They'll never even notice!"

"Now that's using your noggin," Mud Meister said with a grin. "We'll be eating away at that delicious apple tree in no time!"

DIRTY TRICKS

The Mudsters set off to tell Humus about the party. Even though Humus was a Mudster, too, he didn't always fit in. His heart was too big to want to harm living trees. "Remember, we can't tell him that we're going to trick the Treetures," Mud Meister warned.

They found Humus in his kitchen mashing rotten berries.

"Hello, Humus!" Mud Meister said with a slick smile. "You're just the Mudster we've been looking for!"

"Me?" Humus asked. "Really?"

More Than Dirt Dessert

Soil needs lots of layers of ingredients to be healthy—like humus, to give it nutrients and hold moisture; damp mud and sand, to give it structure; and stones, to provide air pockets and drainage so the soil doesn't become too wet.

This delicious chocolate concoction looks just like rich, nutritious soil—and is tons of fun to make and eat! Remember to always get a grown-up's help when using the kitchen.

Ingredients

Chocolate sandwich cookies
(represents the humus layer)
Graham crackers (represents the sandy layer)
Chocolate pudding (represents the mud layer)
Chocolate-covered peanuts or raisins
(represents the stones)
Gummy worms and gummy bugs (healthy
soil is always home to friendly bugs!)
Candy (represents larger stones and can be used
for decoration)

1. Crush the chocolate sandwich cookies into crumbs by placing them between two sheets of waxed paper, then rolling over them with a rolling pin. (Or you can ask an adult to crush them in a food processor.)

2. Then crush the graham crackers into crumbs by hand.

3. In a large glass bowl, start by putting down a layer of chocolate pudding. Then add a layer of the chocolate peanuts or raisins, followed by the chocolate sandwich cookie crumbs, and then the graham cracker crumbs. Be sure to sprinkle a couple gummy worms or bugs between each layer! Repeat until the bowl is full.

4. Decorate the *More Than Dirt Dessert* with candy rocks and more gummy bugs. Yum!

"We're throwing a party at the Stump Dump—and all the Treetures are invited," continued Mud Meister. "Can you whip up their favorite foods so they'll be distracted—I mean, well fed?"

"Of course I can!" he said excitedly. "The Treetures just love my Nitrogen Nuggets, especially with lots of Sweet Soil Sauce. Oh, and I'll have to make some Mineral Mash . . . and Peat Moss Pizza . . . let's see, a big pot of Compost Tea to drink . . . and lots of Crumbly Dirt Cakes for dessert!"

"Sounds delicious!" Mud Meister said. "Now, we have some party planning to do!"

AN INVITATION TO TROUBLE

Later that day, at the Great Oak in Nutley Grove, Twigs, the Treeture Teacher, called all the Treetures together. "I have exciting news, Treetures!" he exclaimed as he unrolled a scroll made out of fallen bark. "The Mudsters are throwing a party at the Stump Dump—and we're all invited!"

"Hooray!" cheered the Treetures.

"Have fun at the party," continued Twigs. "But remember, our job is to be sure that each Mudster rots in the right spots, because good soil makes healthy trees, and healthy trees make a healthier world!"

SEEDS

"The party is tomorrow afternoon, so we'll all have to work especially hard today."

Sprig stepped forward. "I suggest that each Treeture pair up with a Sproutling," he said. "That way we'll have extra help as we work extra hard!"

"Can I come with you, Sprig?" a Sproutling named Chip piped up immediately.

"Of course!" replied Sprig, grinning.

"Good idea, Sprig," added Mama Greenleaf. "Now the Sproutlings will get even more experience in the ways of being a Treeture!"

How can you help the trees in your neighborhood?

CAN'T SEE THE TREE FOR THE PARTY!

For the rest of the afternoon, the Treetures were busier than ever as they checked on all the trees in the magic forest. Rootie and Roothie, the Rooters, cared for all the trees' roots; Chlorophyll and Chlorophyllis helped all the leaves get the sunlight they needed to make tree food; and Woody and Phloemina made sure that sap was flowing freely through the trees. All the while, the Treetures and Sproutlings chattered about the party. They couldn't wait!

But in all the excitement, no one noticed the wound in the apple tree's trunk.

At last it was time for the party.

The Mudsters had truly outdone themselves. The Stump Dump was decorated with streamers made of vines and leaves, and a cluster of fireflies flashed across the dance floor. On a large platform, DK and the Rotten Rockers were jamming. And at the far end of the dump, a long banquet table was crowded with all the treats Humus had made.

"This is going to be the best party ever!" cheered Blossom. "Come on, let's dance!"

PARTY POOPERS

The Treetures crowded onto the dance floor and had a blast dancing to the band. After the first song, Crud shot a sneaky glance at Mud Meister, then put down his saxophone. No one noticed him slip away. Once Crud was out of sight, he rubbed his hands together gleefully. "The plan is working perfectly!" he said. "But I don't want to hang out at the apple tree alone while I wait for the other Mudsters." So Crud invited some of his best insect buds to feast on the tree with him—nasty bugs that would slip into the tree through the wounded trunk and others to snack on the tree's leaves.

Not long after Crud snuck off, Fun Gus followed m.

"Hello, Crud!" Fun Gus called when he reached e apple tree. "It looks like you and your buggy ddies are getting ready for an *excellent* time acking on the tree!"

"We sure are," Crud drooled. "It's going to be licious!"

"Well, just leave enough room for my Bacteria afeteria!" Fun Gus replied. He knew that the ound on the apple tree was the perfect place for rmful bacteria and fungi to enter the tree—and art decomposing it!

BUG MUGS

BAD BUGS

Are there any bad bugs like Crud's friends living in your garden? Use this list to find out!

Gypsy moth
eats tree leaves

Aphid
eats tree leaves and other plants

Mite
eats tree leaves

Caterpillar
eats all kinds of leaves

GOOD BUGS

Bug heroes are everywhere! Find the ones in your garden by using this list.

Ladybug
eats aphids and other plant predators

Worm
enriches the soil

Pill bug
eats decaying plant materials, enriching the soil

Praying mantis
eats plant predators

DISHING THE DIRT

By the time the song finished, only Mud Meister, Root Snoot, and Humus were left onstage. Mud Meister tapped the microphone. "Uh, attention, Treetures," he announced. "DK and the Rotten Rockers will be taking a little break now. Why don't you all head over to the refreshment table where Chef Humus will serve up the food?"

"Come on, Treetures!" Humus exclaimed. "I made all your favorites."

"Everything smells delicious," Twigs said. "Healthy treats for Treetures— or even for trees!"

As the Treetures crowded around Humus, Mud Meister and Root Snoot dashed off to the apple tree.

"Finally!" snorted Root Snoot. "I hate being last to a party! See ya!" And with that, he burrowed deep into the soil to suck up water from the tree's roots.

"Ahhh," said Mud Meister as he dumped a sack of oily muck on the soil around the tree. "This is the life!" The gunk that he added to the soil was very bad for it—now the soil was no longer balanced with just the right nutrients for the tree. But Mud Meister didn't care! He hoped the muck and mud would harden the soil so that water and air couldn't get in to help the roots.

A DIRTY DISCOVERY

Back at the party, the Treetures were happily snacking on all of Humus's specialties. But Chip was distracted. He wanted to visit the apple tree, his favorite tree in all of Nutley Grove! After all, it was caring for the apple tree that had helped the Sproutlings earn their green hearts—the badges they wore proudly that showed the whole world how much they knew about trees.

Without a word, Chip slipped away from the party. *I'll just go visit the tree and come right back,* he thought. *No one will even notice that I'm gone!*

Do you have a favorite tree in your neighborhood?

But when Chip reached the apple tree, a terrible sight met his eyes. Mud Meister was wallowing in muck at the base of the tree. Fun Gus, excited about the squirmy bacteria, was up to no good. And Crud and a group of icky insects were getting ready to feast on the wound on the tree's trunk!

This is awful! Chip thought, his eyes growing wide. *I have to tell the other Treetures!*

A SPROUTLING'S SCARY TALE

Then Chip felt something tap his ankles. He looked down and gasped. Root Snoot's long, snaggly snout was wrapping around his legs and tail!

"Let me go!" cried Chip.

"No way," snarled Root Snoot. "You'll just run off and tell the Treetures what we're up to—and then our fun will be ruined!"

But Chip was too quick for Root Snoot. He hopped from foot to foot, wiggling his legs, until Root Snoot's snout loosened its grip. Then, quick as a flash, Chip darted through the trees back to the Stump Dump.

"Help! Help! Help!" he cried. "The apple tree—the Mudsters—the Mudsters are attacking the apple tree!"

The Treetures gasped.

"What do you mean, Chip?" asked Twigs. "Slow down and tell us everything."

Chip took a deep breath. "There's a wound in the apple tree's trunk, and the Mudsters are attacking it!" he exclaimed.

"We don't have a moment to lose," Sprig announced. "Everyone—to the apple tree!"

TREETURES TO THE RESCUE

"Stop right there!" Sprig yelled to the Mudsters as he ran up to the apple tree. As a Treedom Fighter, Sprig was responsible for protecting all the trees in the forest—especially when they were in danger. He turned to the Treetures and took charge. "The apple tree needs to seal off that wound before things get worse. And we need to help it! Go, Treetures!"

The Treetures scurried into the tree. Together they coaxed the tree into making special chemicals to fight the bacteria. The tree also made a sticky resin, gooey enough to block the bad bugs, bacteria, and fungi. Then the Treetures helped direct the resin to the wound in the bark. Finally, they helped the tree close the edges of the wound to stop the attackers from going deep inside the trunk. Once they were sure the tree was safe, Bugsey took off chasing every bad bug away!

Doc Barkley inspected the Treetures' work. "Well done, everyone!" he exclaimed. "I think the apple tree is going to be just fine. You did it!"

All of the Treetures cheered!

STOMP IT!

"Here I am! Here I am!" Humus yelled breathlessly as he ran into the clearing, pushing the big banquet table filled with party food. "I thought you guys might be hungry, so I brought the party to you!"

But there was still work to be done. One of the Treetures, Stomper, stepped forward. Stomper was a Compost Master. It was his job to make sure there were plenty of fallen leaves, twigs, and branches around each tree in Nutley Grove. The dead tree parts would turn into humus—healthy, vitamin-rich soil to nurture the tree.

"I don't like the looks of this soil," Stomper said in a worried voice. "Someone has poured mucky guck all around this tree! If we can't balance the soil, the tree won't be strong enough to heal its wound—or take care of itself."

FROM MUDSTER TO MUDSTAR!

A worried look crossed Humus's face. He glanced at the soil, then at the table filled with al the delicious food he'd made. Then, in one sudden motion, Humus upended the table!

"Sorry, everybody. I figured maybe the apple tree needed those treats more than the rest of us," Humus said sheepishly, stomping on all the food and mixing it into the soil with his hands.

Stomper grinned at Humus. "Perfect! The peat moss in the pizza will help the soil stay moist—especially important since Root Snoot stole water from the tree. The minerals from th mash and the nitrogen in the nuggets will make the soil rich and healthy. The Sweet Soil Sauc will add the nutrients. And the Crumbly Dirt Cakes will make sure the soil is loose and crumbl so it can drain well. Thanks to you, the tree is getting a lot of what it needs to be healthy."

Sprig stepped forward and pointed to a star on Humus's apron. "Look!" he said. "You're a true Mud *Star*!"

Humus blushed, but everyone could tell he was very pleased.

"My green heart—it's twinkling!" exclaimed Chip.

Twigs smiled. "That's because you did something very important today, Chip," he said. "You helped save the apple tree!"

ROT IN THE RIGHT SPOT!

Then Twigs turned to the other Mudsters. "You all know better than to pick on a healthy tree!" he said sternly. "March right back to the Stump Dump and have your decomposing fun there or on the forest floor—where no living tree will be harmed by it!"

Grumbling, the Mudsters trudged off. Soon the Treetures could hear the sounds of DK and the Rotten Rockers drifting back to Nutley Grove.

"Ahhh, the sounds of good decay happening where it's supposed to," sighed Mama Greenleaf. "That's music to my ears!"

HOME, SWEET HOLLOW

A few magical weeks later, Chip decided to visit the apple tree. A wonderful surprise was waiting for him! The wound was healing nicely, and a small hollow had formed in its place. Best of all, beside the shallow hollow was a small nest—the home to a family of birds!

Chip grinned. He didn't need his green heart to start twinkling again to know how much he'd helped the apple tree—but that's exactly what it did!

Earn a MudSTAR, too!
LEARN TO COMPOST—IT MATTERS!

Did you know that you can compost right at home with things you'd ordinarily throw away? It's easy to do—and a great way to take care of the trees around you!

 Find a quiet spot in your yard, away from your home and direct sunlight. You can compost in a container—like a compost bin you'd find at your local garden supply store—or you can compost right on the ground itself! The best size for a compost pile is about 3 feet wide by 3 feet long by 3 feet tall—not too big and not too small.

 To make compost, you'll need two kinds of organic matter, also known as "brown" and "green" materials. "Brown" materials are dry, and include fallen leaves, small twigs and sticks, shredded paper towels, and straw. "Green" materials are wet, and include grass clippings, fruit and vegetable peels and cores, eggshells, and coffee grounds. Alternate layers of brown and green materials in your compost.

 Once a week, use a shovel or hoe to stir your compost so that air can get in it. Sprinkle water on your compost pile, too, but just enough so that the compost stays damp. No one likes soggy compost—especially not Humus!

In time, with some help from little bugs and bacteria, all the materials you put into the compost pile will become a dark, rich soil, known as humus, that's full of nutrients and vitamins. Sprinkle it around the trees in your yard to help them grow healthy and strong!